How the $\mathcal{S}$ea $\mathcal{M}$arissa Came to

Written by
Anne Renaud

Illustrated by
Maud Durland

Beyond Words Publishing, Inc.

How the Sea Came to Marissa

Anne Renaud

Illustrated by Maud Durland

Beyond Words Publishing, Inc.
20827 N.W. Cornell Road, Suite 500
Hillsboro, Oregon 97124-9808
503-531-8700

Editor: Summer Steele
Proofreader: Jade Chan
Cover and interior design: Jerry Soga

Printed in the United States of America
Distributed to the book trade by Publishers Group West

ISBN 1-58270-129-6

Renaud, Anne.
  How the sea came to Marissa / Anne Renaud ; illustrated by Maud Durland.
    p. cm.
  Summary: Marissa is sad when her visit to Grandma Flora's seaside cottage comes to an end until she finds a way of bringing the sea back with her. Includes instructions for making a sea globe.
  ISBN-13: 978-1-58270-129-5 (hardcover)
  ISBN-10: 1-58270-129-6 (hardcover)
  [1. Seashore—Fiction. 2. Grandmothers—Fiction.] I. Durland, Maud, ill. II. Title.
  PZ7.R28443Ho 2006
  [E]—dc22
                                    2005029986

The corporate mission of Beyond Words Publishing, Inc.:
Inspire to Integrity

To Helena, who always believed.

—Anne Renaud

For my beloved grandchildren, Anton, Beck, & Elsa.

—Maud Durland

Sitting on the front steps of her grandmother's cottage, Marissa looked out at the sea and breathed the salty air that blew in with the tide.

Marissa loved the sea.

She enjoyed wrapping herself with
seaweed to become Wilhelmina
the Sea Witch and scouring the dunes
for lost pirate treasures.
She delighted in chasing the surf
and playing among the waves.

And she always looked forward to building sandcastles that she decorated with crab shells and seagull feathers.

Oh, how Marissa wished she could take a part of the sea home when the time came for her to leave.

After gathering her seashells,
Marissa picked up her bucket and went
inside to see if Grandma Flora was
ready for their evening stroll.

"Why so glum, marzipan?" her grandmother asked as Marissa plopped herself down on a chair at the kitchen table.

"Tomorrow Mom and Dad are coming to take me home," said Marissa, tracing the outline of a small clamshell with her finger. "I have to find a way for the sea to come with me."

"I'm sure you'll think of something," said Grandma Flora, wiping a smudge from the tip of Marissa's nose.

"I know!" Marissa said brightly. "I'll fill my suitcase with sand so I can build sandcastles at home like I did on the beach."

"That might be messy, especially if your cat, Jellybean, mistakes the suitcase for his litter box," Grandma Flora said with a wink.

"Well, I just won't take a bath then. That way, I can smell the sea on my skin and hair whenever I miss it."

"Before long, the sea won't be the only thing you'll be able to smell," chuckled Grandma Flora.

Marissa crinkled her eyebrows and cupped her chin in her hands. "Then I'll catch the sandpipers that race along the shore and keep them in a giant birdcage in my bedroom!"

"But if you take them with you, no one else will be able to enjoy them," said Grandma Flora.

"Then what will I do?" Marissa asked.

Her grandmother draped a yellow cardigan around her shoulders. "Oh, I'm sure you'll think of something, honeybee. Let's go for our walk; it just might bring you some inspiration."

Grandma Flora and Marissa
set out on their evening stroll. On
special nights, they would stop near an
old lighthouse and watch the setting sun
paint the sky in hues of pink and gold.

And when they returned home, the two of
them would often sit on the veranda, curled
up in their pajamas, sipping hot
cocoa with marshmallows and playing
tic-tac-toe or Old Maid.

"I'll find the playing cards and put the
kettle on while you get into your pajamas,"
Grandma Flora said when they arrived back
at the cottage.

"I don't feel like playing a game tonight, Gran,"
Marissa sighed as she plodded off to her bedroom.
"I think I'll just go to bed so I can get up early
and say good-bye to the sea."

After Grandma Flora had tucked her in,
Marissa looked around the room that had
become so familiar to her over the past few
weeks. In the half-light, Marissa's eyes traveled
up the lace curtains, along the dresser with its funny
porthole mirror, and over to the bedside table.

There her stuffed panda sat next to the small snow globe she had found in her grandmother's attic. Marissa took the glass globe in her hand and gave it a light shake. She watched as a flurry of silver sparkles and snowflakes twirled down onto the miniature village below.

When the last snowflake had fallen, Marissa slowly closed her eyes and drifted off to sleep.

The next morning, Marissa awoke with the sun. She dressed quickly and ran down to the shoreline to visit the sea one last time.

As the fresh sea air filled her lungs and the cool grains of sand oozed between her toes, Marissa inspected the many treasures the tide had left behind.

Poking through the garlands of seaweed and fragments of driftwood that had washed up on the beach, Marissa found a round piece of sea glass, polished smooth by water, sand, and time.

"I'm a pirate looking through my spyglass,"
thought Marissa as she held the glass jewel to
her eye. She peered at a hermit crab making
its new home out of an empty snail shell,
then she turned her gaze toward the sea.
Through the pale green lens Marissa spied the
foamy waves rising up onto the shore.

And at that very moment, she had an idea.

"I know how the sea can come with me!" Marissa cried excitedly as she bounded into the kitchen and found her grandmother setting the table for breakfast.

"I knew you'd think of something! And does it involve not washing?" Grandma Flora teased.

"No." Marissa giggled. "But I will need some materials, like a jar and glitter and some glue."

"In that case, we'd best get started. Your parents will be here before we know it."

While Grandma Flora washed out a glass jar and rummaged through her craft box, Marissa laid out the shells she had collected over the summer and began arranging them by size and color.

"Now I need seaweed and some fish. May I pick a few herbs from your garden, Gran?"

"Take whatever you need, especially the weeds and crabgrass," her grandmother joked.

In the backyard Marissa examined the tiny plots of herbs that she and her grandmother had tended every day. As the scent of lavender, rosemary, tarragon, and mint floated up around her, Marissa carefully made her selection. After gathering what she needed, the garden's sweet fragrances followed her back inside.

"Heavens, what will you do with those?"
Grandma Flora asked when Marissa came
in carrying a handful of tiny pebbles and
sprigs of fennel and baby dill.

"It's a surprise," said
Marissa as she busied
herself with sorting
and gluing.

When she finished filling
the jar with seashells,
pebbles, glitter,
herbs, and water,
Marissa announced,
her face beaming,
"TA-DA! Can you guess
what this is, Gran?"

Before Grandma Flora could guess, Marissa gave
the jar a light shake and exclaimed, "It's a sea globe!
Now the sea can come with me, and I can hold it in
my hands whenever I miss it."

And that's exactly what she did.
And *that's* how the sea came to Marissa.

Sea Globe Instructions

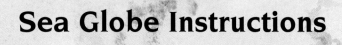

- To make your very own sea globe you will need:
- A grownup's help
- A small glass jar (a round jar works best)
- A glue gun
- Seashells (small and medium sizes, depending on the size of your jar)
- Several sprigs of herbs
- Eggshells (thoroughly cleaned and dried overnight)
- Small pebbles (optional)
- Glitter (any color)
- Water
- Baby oil (optional)

1. Thoroughly wash out a small glass jar.
2. Glue the seashells to the center of the inside of the jar lid and set it aside to dry for at least 20 minutes to an hour. (Helpful hint: After gluing each shell, check to make sure the lid still fits the jar securely.)
3. To make seaweed, use sprigs of herbs, such as baby dill, rosemary, or fennel. If you don't have any herbs, cut small strips from a green garbage bag.
4. To make fish, crush tiny seashells or eggshells with a rolling pin. Or you may use small pebbles.
5. Add your crushed shells (or pebbles), seaweed, and glitter to the empty jar.
6. Fill the jar with water and screw the lid on tightly. To slow down the movement of the objects inside the jar and to make them "float," substitute the water with baby oil.
7. Turn the jar upside down and shake it gently.

Now you have your very own sea to visit whenever you wish!